A Battleaxe and a Metal Arm 13:

The Abyssal Machine

Samuel Fleming

Thank you to my Beta Readers

and to my First Reader,

Mel.

Contents

"So many long to suffer
immortality… They know not
what they ask."
—nameless

Previously...

The heroes and Idnauthi survivors found themselves in a frozen, wind-torn realm. In one direction lay the Godpeak, to the other lay a village. Helesys kindled warmth for the group, stretching her powers nearly to their limits, and they trekked across the hills to the village.

Their first encounter with the villagers was a buried trap meant to keep others away, but they convinced the villagers to allow them passage and sanctuary. They were brought to the old village of Lamoral, carved from the ice and bolstered by magic. They were offered food, warmth, and solace for the night.

In the quiet of the longhouse, they spoke of the visages that Mr. Mask used against them. Helesys felt that her sister Aradi had tried to kill her. Taunauk felt that his father was dead. Shawn felt that he had lived with the grandfather and the young boy, but they were not his kin.

Helesys, Taunauk, and Shawn, spoke with the elder O'Ten, and she confided in them. They spoke of their gift to bring treasures back beyond death, of failure of the other chosen to defeat the Wolf King, and of the answers to be found on the Godpeak. O'Ten confessed that the path up the mountain was treacherous, but that did not deter the heroes.

In the morning, the heroes and the Idnauthi survivors parted ways. The survivors would stay in the village and live among the people, and after heartfelt goodbyes, the heroes set out across the snowy hills.

Along the way, they found strange creatures that stood as icy Terrans with towering antlers, and were attacked by a giant manta ray that swam beneath the ice. Weapons could not crack its scaly hide, but Helesys stretched her power to hold the creature and then to control it—a feat she'd seen the Wolf King and Sigun do before. Though she managed to drive the creature to the base of the mountain, the power sickened her, and she resolved not to use it again.

Soon after, they found the entrance to the inner passages of the mountain, and found the layout one both magical and designed by intelligent hands—the culmination of which they would find on the summit: That the mountain was made of powerful, old magic similar to the god serpent Shéslang.

They met resistance in the mountain: The bloody remnants of cursed cannibal creatures—Wendigos. Helesys tried to hold the creatures, but instead saw memory of the grisly fate that befell the travelers. Such cursed things could not be bound. In the end, Helesys called upon a newfound spell of fire while Taunauk and Shawn cleaved the creatures.

When they stopped to rest, Taunauk told them more of Endroggen rage—he talked of the training of warriors and soldiers, and of killing intent, but that rage was all those things and more. Endroggen were craftsmen of emotions and memories, forging them into weapons to be harnessed in times of need.

Further in, they found another beast—a massive centipede made of both icy shell and fiery blood. Their weapons could not penetrate it, and the beast grew sweltering hot—so much that it melted Taunauk's axe. It spewed magma over them, but the Ring of Winter protected them. It grew so hot that the cavern collapsed.

And from the walls, a giant owl woke from its icy slumber—its body clear and wings silent. It fought off the centipede in a titanic battle, then gathered the heroes and took them to the summit of the Godpeak.

The owl's name was Kuatari, and its past life, its kind had been guardians of a forest. But now they were trapped in the dungeon, like so many other Terrans and gods. It too had seen chosen like them, and echoed their failures—that the Wolf King lived.

It left them to their memories upon the Godpeak. There, Taunauk found three dozen Endroggen spirits—one of which was his father, Rehkoros. Rehkoros revealed that the dungeon had appeared in Accaelum and trapped ten thousand Endroggen souls. The elders had seen omens of such a powerful event, and had chosen the young child, Taunauk, to be raised as a champion of the people, but one denied connections to the mortal realm so that he could be a vessel of souls when the time came. Taunauk's purpose was to find the dungeon, then find the ten thousand souls of his people and free them. While he and his father tentatively reconnected, Taunauk realized that finding them and escaping meant he would lose his father forever.

Helesys saw memories of her mother and sister again, and the visions left her with still more questions. Helesys heard her own voice responding to her mother, that she 'had lost everything in the war'. Then heard herself again talking to Aradi. In spite of her sister's lies, Aradi had been by her side in recovery, and that she had found something for her—something that Helesys sought desperately but was still locked behind her memories.

And in the aftermath, Shawn had his own realizations. He discovered why he was neither elven nor human—he was a wisp from the plane of dreams. The black wrappings around his arms were bindings that held his form, and undone his form became ghostly. Shawn drifted from the Godpeak, vanishing through the seam and across other realms.

In the end, sorrow for Shawn's absence gave way to resolve—that Helesys and Taunauk would continue their course. They would return to Zhug's realm and seek his aid. Then they would dive beneath the waves to find the Machine of Antrikaumora.

~ ~ ~

Return to Zhug

Icy wind whipped at the heroes atop the Godpeak as Helesys Byyra reached out with her magics and opened the seam between worlds. She sought the castle—the dungeon— and the ancient barracks deep within it. Long forgotten by soldiers and reclaimed by goblins and the giant, Zhug.

She found the castle easily. It pervaded the realms, blotting out the sky and casting many in perpetual night and the rest in eternal dusk. And in each it was dizzying to stare at, the walls climbing up to impossible heights, and the spires above seeming to pierce the sky.

The familiar dusty starting room was next, and then she sought the branching path that led to the barracks.

She smiled—it was fitting that they were returning. Zhug had been the first to recognize them as Chosen, and had been the first to aid them, though reluctantly. He had watched them carefully that first time, let them fight his minions—tested them.

How would Zhug receive them this time, she wondered.

~

Helesys and Taunauk stepped through the seam, the wind of the Godpeak becoming mute, frozen summit giving way to stagnant, musty air.

The weaver sighed deeply, overcome by a sudden weariness.

This was the second realm they had appeared in, and her mind reeled at the psychic distance. Only scant few deaths separated that first visit from this, and they had learned much in that short time—much more than other denizens did in five times as many lives.

Yet, she and Taunauk were not the same. Even without the heavy realizations of the Godpeak, they were not the same weaver and barbarian who had walked those quiet halls. The dungeon had changed them, remade them—or perhaps, Helesys and Taunauk had remade themselves.

It was the silence, she'd decided. For those first few realms, Helesys and Taunauk had been tentative comrades, journeying together because they had no one else. They had walked in silence for much of those early realms, doing so out of caution for danger and weariness of each other. Bound together in desperation and necessity.

Yet there had been echoes of familiarity even then, and now she could think of no one else she'd rather journey with, save for Shawn.

Helesys looked to her comrade and found him stoic and intently staring at the torches on the wall. He walked over and, in one easy motion, ripped the sconce from the wall. Stone scattered across the ground.

They walked down the dusty, torch-lit hallway, their footsteps echoing in the silence.

~

It wasn't long before Helesys had the feeling of being watched. It was heavy and loomed over them—the touch of a powerful mage who did not hide their power.

She smiled and turned toward the scrying eye of the mage. It hung above them, some ten feet away, near the ceiling of the hall. Helesys *felt* there was an outline, the vaguest circular shape against the stone, but she couldn't be sure if her eyes were seeing anything or if it was her latent magical sense.

Taunauk, too, was staring at the scrying eye as if he could see it, though Helesys had no idea how the barbarian was sensing its presence.

"So, you've come back." The giant's gravelly voice rumbled through the hall.

"We need your help," Helesys said. "We were told to seek you, that you have a contraption that can get us beneath the endless sea."

A thoughtful grumble echoed through the hall. "Come to me," Zhug said. "Stizzai and the others will let you pass. Come to my throne room and we will have words."

The hall grew quiet and the scrying presence faded, but it did not disappear. Helesys still felt as if they were being watched—she knew it was Zhug, yet she hadn't felt such a subtle touch from him.

For a breath, she nearly asked why, but she decided it wouldn't help. No matter what Zhug thought of their return—whether he was curious or apprehensive—they needed his help.

Both she and Taunauk walked the hall without weapons drawn or magic ready.

~

Their first time in the realm, they had passed rooms of wreckage, broken furniture and piled metal. But now they were met by goblins. The tiny Terrans stood at attention along the hall. Their skin was mottled greens and yellows, covered in patches of black hair.

Though Helesys nodded to several of them, they did not return her greeting. They merely watched with curious stares at these Terrans who were permitted into the realm.

As they passed, Helesys looked for a single goblin among them—Widewill, the outcast.

It wasn't until they had passed several rooms that they came to a wiry goblin that was smiling.

"*Helesys! Taunauk!*" Widewill stepped forward to greet them. Then he turned to the other goblins and added, "*Don't be afraid. She is a good weaver.*"

Helesys smiled at him, her wand-arm humming with translation, and said, "*Widewill, you're no longer an outcast?*"

Though Taunauk could not understand the goblin, he smiled warmly as well.

Widewill shook his head frantically. "*No. Zhug has forgiven me. I'm a goblin again.*"

At that, goblins began grumbling around them. The two nearest backed away from Widewill, as if there were those that didn't accept his return.

"*Leave Widewill be and let the Terrans pass,*" Zhug's voice echoed from above. Then to Helesys and Taunauk, Zhug said, "Follow the hall and do not delay."

Widewill's stature diminished, but his smile remained. "*You should go. Zhug waits for no Terran.*"

Helesys nodded. As heartwarming as it was to see the small Terran, she found no words. She merely said, "Thank you," and, "Farewell."

As she and Taunauk walked past the rest of the goblins, she hoped that little Widewill would find peace amongst his brethren.

~

They walked the halls, mindful of the traps marked and held aside by goblins. At the end of the hall, a small group of goblins greeted them. These were clad in full armor. The pauldrons and greaves were oversized—clearly made for humans or elves.

Stizzai stood at their front, tall, proud, and fearsome. Tailored armor sat atop her thick shoulders. Tusks jutted out of a disapproving glare. It was impossible to tell if she had scars from the last encounter, for they were innumerable.

The sight of the goblin leader made Helesys pause. Though it had been ten realms since their last encounter, Helesys would not forget that perilous encounter in the Z-shaped hall. Stizzai had nearly been too much for both her *and* Taunauk.

And just behind the group stood Zhug's metal men—torchlight reflecting in their obsidian armor. Each held a giant warhammer. Soulless and bodiless, they'd been nearly invulnerable—*nearly*. Helesys and Taunauk had damaged them, but both were immaculate once more.

Silence hung in the air, and finally, Stizzai growled. "Follow me."

~

They walked the rest of the halls, surrounded by the soldiers. The metal men flanked them front and back, their armor near silent save for soft clicking of plates. Stizzai walked in front.

Helesys smirked. It was an eerily similar procession to the first time they met Zhug.

It was a notion quickly forgotten as they passed the telltale trap door in the first large room—the entrance to the crypt where the Many-Handed Horror, Shomosk dwelled.

Of all the fates in Zhug's realm, that was the one she did not wish to revisit.

They walked the final hall and pushed open the large doors to Zhug's throne room.

Treasures beyond imagination filled the room and lined the halls: Mantles of weapons and jewelry, rows of colored potions, strange contraptions, and between it was a landscape of piles of gold coins.

Twice now, Helesys had seen Zhug's horde of treasure, and twice she'd been awestruck at the sight of it.

She turned to the left and found the giant sitting atop an equally massive throne—the stone crunching beneath Zhug's weight as he shifted. He wore a patchwork shirt of animal skins, his mottled skin peeking out from beneath it. In his left hand, he held three magic staves in between his fingers; these he pointed at the heroes.

Zhug regarded them. One eye bloodshot and weary, the other glass—his scrying eye. Again, Helesys couldn't help but notice his many earrings, and the single magical one in particular. Though the others were ornate and exquisitely crafted, that one was encrusted with purple jewels.

Zhug grumbled. "Leave us, Stizzai." Then he beckoned for the heroes to approach his throne.

The goblin leader glared at Helesys and Taunauk a moment before turning and leaving. The obsidian soldiers, however, followed Helesys and Taunauk.

Zhug's red eye fell to each of them in turn. "Back so soon. So very soon."

"You expected us," Helesys said.

Zhug nodded. "It was only a matter of time before you learned to walk between the realms."

Helesys smirked. "Something you conveniently forgot to mention. How many other things could you have told us?"

The giant shrugged. "You would've found your answers, eventually. Even the tenacious mind can only concern itself with one truth at a time. I told you what you needed to know. So, weaver, what have you learned in your travels?"

Helesys and Taunauk told Zhug of their journey: Of meeting Amadeus and their brush with the Wolf King. Of learning to walk across the seams of the worlds. Of the Voice at Meridian who bid them to find the Machine of Antrikaumora, and of the god serpent Shéslang and the other Chosen, and of One-Mind. Then of the Godpeak, but silence fell when it came time to say what they found on the mountain.

Zhug smiled widely and rubbed his scratchy chin. "So much in so short a time. Perhaps there's hope for you yet where the other Chosen have failed. Perhaps the Wolf King's reign is at an end. And so the Voice bid you to return here, and this Voice is the source of your power."

Taunauk spoke up, "You sound surprised by that."

Zhug nodded. "There are not many secrets left for my ears. Amadeus and I had our suspicions about the Chosens' powers. He thought they were anomalies—random chance." The giant smiled. "There are no anomalies. There is no fate but what we make for ourselves."

Helesys said, "The Machine lies at the bottom of the ocean. Miles beneath the surface. Will you aid us once more?"

Zhug flicked his wrist, and there was a scraping of metal. Helesys turned to see the massive metal crab half-walking, half-floating toward them. It's eight legs scraped the piles of gold, and it landed hard beside Taunauk.

"This will suffice," it said.

Helesys and Taunauk looked over the hulk of metal. Its form was a crude approximation of a crab. A bulky body sat atop spindly legs with two pincer claws. The metal was sleek and seamless—clearly crafted by something arcane.

Zhug continued, "There is enough room for you both to sit inside. It is designed so that the controls can be operated by two or three Terrans. It's completely watertight and the air inside regenerates."

With another flick of his staff, the crab lowered its body to the floor, showing a hatch on top of the main body.

"The words are *emarces* and *cresce*, *shrink* and *enlarge*," Zhug added.

Helesys reached out with her gauntlet and tried the first word. With the sound of crunching metal, the submersible shrunk down to the floor and became no bigger than the palm of her hand.

She picked it up and turned the cold metal over in her gauntlet, the two metals clinking softly against one another. She eyed the giant curiously, but Taunauk gave breath to her question first.

"Why are you helping us, Zhug?" Taunauk asked.

"Not that we mind," Helesys added.

The giant grumbled and waved a dismissive hand. "You can see clearly that I have no use for it." But despite his attitude, Helesys could plainly see worry on his face.

Memory of their first meeting echoed in her head: *If you die a thousand deaths and find yourselves in my halls again… If you find yourself set against me and hold my life in your hands… Grant me mercy.*

Had he merely not wanted to die by their hands and be reborn without his horde? The loss of all his power would be tragic, but what artifact could the giant lose that he could not reclaim? Surely a mage could find all those things again, especially if he could walk between the seams…

Perhaps Zhug had been imprisoned without any magic items at all. A mage reborn without a wand—now that would be cause for concern.

Helesys had been about to ask Zhug for the truth, but saw plainly in his bloodshot eye that he wouldn't answer her.

Instead, Helesys placed the tiny metal crab in her pack, and she said, "You weren't surprised by the Godpeak… and you didn't ask what we found on the summit. We found spirits and memories. What did you find up there?"

The giant laughed, low and rumbling like distant thunder. "Is that the best question you could think of, weaver?"

Helesys said plainly, "Just the most interesting."

Zhug regarded her and his mirth faded. She felt the lingering presence of his scrying eye watching her as well.

"I found memories. Distant, primal, and almost incomprehensible…" Zhug trailed off, as if lost in recollection. "Have you become someone else yet, weaver, outlander?"

Helesys and Taunauk shared a look of curiosity, but neither answered readily.

Finally, Helesys said, "It's hard to say what we've become when we still don't remember what we were."

Again, Zhug waved a dismissive hand. "Amadeus said the same thing. Without your memories, you *are* someone different. Even when you regain them, you won't be the same. This place has changed you."

Helesys smiled softly—something that did not go unnoticed.

"Something funny, weaver?"

"I just didn't take you for the philosophical type. The thought of you and Amadeus sitting in his spire is... wholesome."

Zhug slumped back on his throne. "Amadeus is a dear friend, prone to such thoughts. He thinks my *stature* gives me a unique insight."

When the giant didn't elaborate further, Helesys asked, "Is there anything you can tell us about the Machine or about the journey to it? How will we find it down there?"

Zhug replied, "Such things leave a mark on the world. Call it an aura or an indentation or a presence—you will feel it as surely as you feel the seams."

"Have you been down there?"

Zhug shook his head. "I can't fit in the metal crab, but I've heard stories of strange creatures and ruins on the bottom of the sea. Once you reach those ruins, the lingering magic will sustain you without breath. That there are even stranger things inside the ruins than there are at the bottom of the sea."

Taunauk added, "More lost worlds."

The giant nodded. "This world is an abyss, outlander, and all that are trapped within are sinking deeper into it, sifting through the realms. All to be lost and eventually buried. If you were to dig you would find the ashes of a million civilizations buried beneath the dungeon—do not become one of them.

"Now, go," Zhug said with a wave of his massive hand, "before I send you wandering. And if we meet again, I shall take it that you've failed."

Helesys felt magic swell in the room—that there was a seam in the treasure room. It had been there the entire time, hidden by Zhug's magic.

Helesys stared up at the giant, other questions swirling within her—some of which were about Zhug. She thought of all those lost civilizations, all of those histories lost and buried. Zhug and Amadeus and the others had pasts just as rich. And the weaver felt a pang of sadness that she would not know the giant better.

She pushed away the thought and reached out for the seam, searching for ocean salt and sand. She found it and pulled open the seam easily.

Zhug smiled at her prowess. "Farewell, Helesys and Taunauk."

The weaver and the outlander echoed his words. They stepped through the seam, leaving their ally and the barracks behind.

~ ~ ~

Diving Beneath the Endless Sea

Helesys and Taunauk stepped through the seam. The cool air of the underground gave way to sun and sand, and the smell of salt.

They were alone on the beach. Helesys closed her eyes and felt the warmth of the sun upon her face. With it came the memory of walking the dunes with Taunauk, finding Shawn, and sailing aboard the *Malorienta* together.

Sand scrunched beneath her boots, and the giant's words echoed in her head: *All of those histories—all of those Terrans—lost and buried.*

"Not us," Helesys muttered.

Taunauk stared at her.

"It won't be us," she said. "We won't be buried in this place. We won't fail."

Her comrade nodded slightly, then turned back to the sea. At times, Taunauk could be too quiet—he could be every bit the abyss that the dungeon was. He seemed even quieter since the Godpeak.

Helesys said, "Now I know what I looked like when I talked to my wand."

The outlander smirked. "It was very apparent."

"Do your ancestors speak to you?"

"Sometimes. Sometimes they speak to each other, and I'll hear their whispers. It's as if I'm carrying a piece of Accaelum with me."

"That sounds beautiful."

"It is."

But there was a bitterness in his voice—a shadow of pain.

Helesys asked, "How are you holding up?"

"My whole life has been in preparation for this place, for saving the souls of my people." Taunauk breathed deep.

"Did you need some time? You just found your father—"

"We should get moving." Taunauk's voice was level and calm—a mask for his turmoil.

Helesys sensed this, and though she wanted to ask more, she pulled out the metal crab from her pocket and set it on the sand. Then she spoke the magic words to bring it back to its normal size.

With a long screech of metal and several clangs, the device grew. A moment later, the dark metal was tall and staring vacantly back at them.

Helesys walked around the side and climbed up the footholds on its flank. As she peered over the top, a circular hatch opened—smooth and silent except for a quiet hiss. The inside glowed a deep red, highlighting levers and switches that stuck at odd angles like some infernal skeleton.

"Here goes," she muttered, and climbed inside. Her boots echoed dully as she touched the floor, and she noticed that the hatch above widened slightly as she passed through. Not only that, but the Gar of Shéslang shortened before her eyes; at first she thought it a trick of the light, but it must have been the magic of the diving machine.

Inside, there were five seats, two in the front and three in the back. The controls were arranged around the front two seats.

Taunauk's steps echoed through the metal and a moment later he was climbing through the hatch. The hole widened enough to accommodate Everfall, and a few moments later, Everfall and the axe were both shortening so that they would comfortably fit inside the room.

Instead of ducking, both heroes sat in the front two seats. As they did, there was a low whine of metal as levers and switches reoriented—twisting and bending so that they were within reach of the occupants.

Helesys saw the artisanship in the metal, and thought of what her wand had once said, that most magic items weren't alive, not in such a sense—that most were little more than tools.

Helesys turned inward to her wand, and asked, *Are you there?*
I am always with you, Helesys Byyra.
Do you sense a presence in the diving machine?
It is rudimentary. A magic item built for a singular purpose. Why do you ask?
Just curious.

The metal shell of the front of the crab was equally strange. Out of the corner of her eye, the walls appeared the same dark gray metal, but when Helesys looked directly at the front, the metal turned transparent. It felt as if she were staring through tissue paper, the beach and shoreline veiled with thin tapestry.

Helesys had been about to ask her wand what each lever did, but as the elf reached for the controls, she *felt* what each one did. There were two especially intricate mechanisms, one in front of her and Taunauk—these were for the twin pincer arms. Most other levers controlled the legs, while switches alternated between swimming and walking motions. Helesys sensed that with these the machine would switch without their input. The last few levers controlled buoyancy and emergency actions.

Helesys explained the mechanisms to Taunauk, and then they both pulled corresponding levers to turn the crab toward the sea. Helesys breathed a sigh of relief as the crab walked into the water, for it seemed that magic did much on its own; all they had to do was direct the crab, and the levers that controlled the legs began moving in unison without a Terran's hand.

Taunauk, however, wore a look of barely concealed disdain.

"You don't approve?" Helesys asked as the crab marched toward the water. The legs became rhythmic thumps on the sand.

"Sorcery," Taunauk grumbled.

The crab crossed into the waves and didn't stutter as they broke on its front. It pressed on—they pressed on, and soon they were completely submerged.

Blue sky gave way to murky green. Above them, sunlight shimmered on the rolling waves. The lull of the shallows echoed through the metal in long groans. They followed the downward slope of the dunes until the sound of the waves and the light of the sun grew distant.

And as the light from above faded, the red light from within the crab grew until everything was blood and shadow. The red light extended out like a gory torch. Schools of tiny fish darted past them, pursued by three larger, snake-like fish.

Taunauk had been silent and tense since they left dry land, and only then began to breathe steadily. Helesys thought back to the deck of the *Malorienta* when Taunauk had nearly given in to the sirens' song and lept overboard—Helesys still vividly remembered her comrade's fear of drowning.

Helesys asked, "Are you sure you're alright?"

"Better now. I don't like this—being underwater."

The weaver thought back to their last trip underwater, when they were nearly to One-Mind's core—when they had fought the renegade automaton, Dissimul.

"You seemed alright during our journey through One-Mind's realm."

Taunauk sighed. "One-Mind's magic was far beyond this contraption. This seems flimsy in comparison. And back then, I did not have the fate of my ancestors upon my shoulders."

Helesys nodded. "But you did, Taunauk. You just didn't know it."

"My first point still stands."

She smiled. "You're right. One-Mind was a master of the realm." Then she added, "I wonder what Shawn would think of this contraption?"

"That's probably why he left."

The weaver and barbarian shared a quiet laugh. In the distance, a stark line appeared—a cliff's edge. Murky sand gave way to red void.

Beside her, Taunauk squeezed the hilt of his axe.

"What's the matter, Taunauk?" She asked, trying to lighten the mood. "Too soon for us to die?"

"I want to die fighting something."

The crab stepped over the cliff, and there was a moment of silence as they hung in the air. Then Helesys's stomach dropped.

A moment later, a lever moved on its own, and the crab lurched forward and started swimming. Its legs trailed behind it, and its body lurching gently from side-to-side.

Just as Helesys regained her composure, the crab turned and dove into the depths.

An underwater landscape passed them like they were flying. Great flowing corals grew atop bulbous outcroppings of rocks—all manner of tiny fish darted between them. Even in the red light of the crab, Helesys could see the myriad of colors and shades of diversity. Lazy sharks swum above them, patrolling these thresholds for larger game.

As the heroes pressed deeper and deeper, the corals changed several times; long tendrils gave way to fans and frills. Eels peeked out from the rocks. Schools of fish grew in both size and breadth until they loomed overhead like clouds in the void.

The bellow of a giant sea turtle rattled the hull as they passed. The shell of the creature was three times the size of their magic craft, and covered in algae that highlighted the gouges in its shell. Clusters of cleaning fish swam alongside like hungry specters.

Deeper still, they passed towers that rose up from the floor. The tops billowed deadly mixes of steam and sulfur—just passing near was enough for the hull to grow hot and the rotten smell to seep through. So Helesys grasped the directional level and gently guided the crab around the towers.

~

Soon even the smoke towers disappeared, and the sea floor seemed to drop off as if they'd passed beyond a cliff's edge. The world was red around them as they plunged into the unknown. It was some time before both weaver and barbarian relaxed their grips on the gar and the axe.

Beside her, Taunauk's eyes were closed and his face was hard in concentration. His lips moved slightly, as if he was dreaming or talking silently to himself. She couldn't tell if these were prayers of fortitude or if he was talking to the spirits within him.

Helesys sought to fill the silence. So rather than disturb Taunauk, she turned inward.

She said inwardly to her wand, *I have questions about magic items.*

Ask them.

You said that most magic items aren't sentient. They don't have minds. They don't speak. The Gar of Shéslang seems different. I feel it sometimes in battle—it revels in battle. But other than that it is quiet.

Her wand replied, *The spear was already powerful when it was made, but then it was stuck in the body of the God Serpent. We have seen powerful beings warp their realms—some by acting, others just by their sheer presence. By being embedded in Shéslang, the spear was changed, warped—deepened.*

You're saying that the spear became sentient from being stuck in Shéslang?

Yes, though sentient may be a stretch. Shawn's coin is not sentient. Zhug's metal men are not sentient.

Helesys said, *Maybe 'awake' is a better term?*

That is a sufficient distinction.

The weaver was silent for a moment. She had so many questions and did not know where to start.

Her wand spoke up, *You're going to ask if I was sentient—truly sentient—in our life before.*

Helesys shifted in her seat. *How did you know?*

Just as you can sense my direction and my warnings without words, I can sense your thoughts, too.

So, were you sentient before?

The wand hesitated. *I think so.*

Were you different? Did you awaken in one of the realms while we've been imprisoned?

I have always been different. Always sentient. I could not speak to you before because a connection was severed.

Helesys nodded slightly, though she wasn't sure if her wand could feel the gesture. She remembered the connection that One-Mind fixed—something that had been severed long before she had been imprisoned in the dungeon. She still felt that it was some kind of sabotage, even if she couldn't fully explain it.

Helesys asked her wand, *Why did you hesitate when I asked if you were sentient?*

I don't feel that you listened as well as you do now—you did not heed my warnings and my direction.

That's silly. Why would a soldier not listen to their wand if they could?

I do not know, Helesys. I wish I could remember more. For now, It is only a feeling. Do not trouble yourself.

Helesys eyed her gauntlet as it rested on the chair, metal against metal, and magic coursing through both. She felt camaraderie and warmth.

Had it really been such a short time ago that her wand was silent? Nothing more than feelings, like the Gar of Shéslang. Now, the weaver could scarcely imagine not speaking to her wand, could scarcely imagine the silence.

Helesys glanced over and saw Taunauk's mouth moving slightly, watching him a moment while he spoke with the spirits within. She smiled at the thought of them, both alone in this strange and hostile world, and speaking with the things inside their heads instead of each other.

The weaver finally said to her wand, *You're clearly special. Thank you for speaking to me.*

I am with you always, Helesys Byyra. And I am grateful.

~

In the abyss, there was nothing to mark their passage—no landmarks, no day or night, no stars. Time seemed to stop.

Helesys looked to her comrade and found Taunauk staring off into the dim red glow.

She asked, "Have you spoken more to the spirits?" Taunauk nodded, and she asked, "Have you learned anything more from them?"

It was a moment before he answered. "There are more than just Endroggen."

"But weren't the spirits on the Godpeak from Accaelum?"

Taunauk smiled softly. "Not all of them. Three are different: One is a human from one thousand years ago, so old he's forgotten nearly everything save for his name; his people lived in the desert, using rage to sustain them where sustenance was meager. Second is a four armed centaur we saw statues of in the cannibal jungle; rage was a tool of their warriors. Third is a made-thing Terran created by the crystal beings beneath the Hive—it learned rage on its own and without teaching."

Helesys tried to contain her excitement. "So it is possible for another to learn blood magic!"

Taunauk nodded tentatively.

She asked, "How did they discover it on their own?"

The barbarian hesitated. "You will not like the answer." But when Helesys wasn't deterred, Taunauk continued, "The made-thing was barely a Terran when it was conceived. It was without reason—nearly an animal. It was little more than flesh and bone possessed by pure emotion.

"It taught itself to control those feelings—*it had to learn*, otherwise such a powerful storm would've torn the poor Terran asunder."

Helesys turned back to the red void in front of her. "You don't think it's possible for a normal Terran to master… How do children learn then?"

"Some of it is passed down in the blood; some of it is taught. The children start young. It is the only way to learn."

Helesys turned to him. "Would you teach me?"

Taunauk turned to face her as well, eyes narrowed in question. There was a flicker of gold in his eyes, and his lips moved as if he were speaking to the spirits. When a long moment had passed, his eyes returned to their normal brown.

"I have spoken with the elder spirits," he said. "They have never known a Terran to learn our rage, but… My father is grateful for your aid, and I confessed that if any other Terran has the prowess and the will necessary to learn it, it is you. Help me find the other lost spirits of Accaelum, and I will teach you Endroggen rage."

Helesys breathed a sigh of relief. Even though blood magic was sacred to the Endroggen, the weaver had been prepared to beg for the opportunity to learn. Thankfully, the elder spirits had seen to reason.

Her thoughts drifted to the Wolf King, to his powerful display as he broke through the wards and magics of Amadeus's tower. That day, the King had not just broken through but also psychically fought her and Amadeus.

Helesys had seen many awesome realms, terrible creatures, and wondrous powers in their journey through the dungeon, but that early battle in the wizard's tower still sent a shiver through her.

She knew that if they had any hope of defeating the Wolf King and winning their freedom, they would need every power and advantage that they could muster.

And that meant that Helesys very much needed to learn Endroggen rage.

~

They continued down through the sea. Occasionally, a thin fish or a pulsing jelly would shine red in their lights. Another time, they saw the flank of something in the distance, and as the metal crab swam closer and closer, the flank of the creature grew until it blotted out the void with a deep green—a gargantuan scaled whale with a flank that shimmered like broken glass.

When they were alone again in the ocean void, Helesys asked, "What is my first lesson?"

Taunauk smirked. "I've never taught someone how to harness their rage… What do you feel when you fight?"

"I feel empty. Like my mind gives way to my soldier's training. I act with purpose, but training guides me. Back in the tunnels of the Godpeak, you told us how harnessing rage was like being a blacksmith and a warrior. I do not feel like either— I feel like the sword. Like the weapon… Nothing like when I felt your rage."

"But you are still in control," Taunauk replied.

"...I suppose."

"You are *always* in control. I remember a weaver who spoke of how easily violence came to her, and how she struggled not to visit violence upon all those who got in her way. You have a choice between violence and peace, just as you have a choice between which spells to use against an opponent. You may have a soldier's training, but your body and your gauntlet are the weapons—you are in control. You dictate how they are used."

Helesys considered her comrade's words. She knew them to be true, but it was difficult to think back to the moments of battle and remember how they happened—like trying to catch the first bursts of flame from a spark. Where did her mind— her choice—end and the blade begin?

"What of choice?" she asked. "I often do not have a choice in the spells that I choose. There are clearly optimal choices against certain foes."

Taunauk grunted in dissatisfaction. "We are ill-prepared for philosophy. Remember, Helesys of House Byyra, *you are not the weapon.* This is your first teaching."

Helesys smiled at the echo of her own words—they hadn't broached philosophy since the wode.

"Thank you," the weaver said quietly.

~

The heroes and the metal crab dove deeper and deeper into the void and Helesys felt the growing pull of magic, as if they were slipping over the edge of a chasm and into a pit. It seemed to tug at their vessel, pulling them at ever increasing speed.

Her wand whispered quietly, *We are nearly there.*

Moments later, they came upon huge, dark metal spires. These shimmered in the weak light of the crab like red specters and passed as silently. Several towers stood alone, but others stood in clusters, as if they'd once been joined together with now-splintered walkways. Long ribbon-thin eels gathered on the flanks of the monuments like shredded tapestries.

The metal around them began to groan long and slow. Taunauk grunted and eyed their surroundings.

The pressure outside is changing, her wand said. *The spires are growing more numerous and so is the magic.*

With her wand's voice came more towering structures—these were a pinkish white, starkly contrasted with the others. As they neared the first of these new pillars, Helesys's gauntlet hummed with warning. She saw suckers along the side of it and a patchwork of thin blue veins beneath it. As Helesys reached for the controls, the firsts of the enormous tentacles turned and reached for them—as if a pale forest was collapsing around them.

The heroes dove, the crab weaving a treacherous path down and through the tentacles. Helesys and Taunauk lurched in their seats and held tightly to the levers. But for every length they evaded, it seemed as if three more took their place. Their evasion became frantic, the crab pitching and lurching violently.

Helesys reached out for the creature, hoping that there was something she could do from within the confines.

"Restu sonmova, krakanis."

In realms past, she had used the holding spell on creatures both large and terrible. Made-things had little mind to hold and they did not know fear. Lower creatures were solely dependent on their size to protect from such a spell. More powerful mages and Terrans recognized the mental attack for the spell that it was and could counter it as a fighter parries an attack.

Since Helesys's wand-arm had been repaired by One-Mind, her power had grown. In the last realm, she had held the giant manta ray *and* controlled it—a feat she would've thought impossible before.

But as she shared mindspace with the kraken, as she glimpsed its looming, twisted shadow, Helesys once again felt small. A wall of flesh loomed in the darkness of the endless sea, writhing and unafraid of the weaver's pitiful grasp.

The forest of tentacles grew, dozens more sprouting from the seafloor—a wall of white.

Helesys flared her kindled power, compounding it with the Gar of Shéslang. "*Restu sonmova, krakanis!*"

And in the mindspace, Helesys grew until she too was a giant. She stared back against the writhing veil of darkness and forced it to come into the light—something not of their world. Hundreds of eyes glistened like stars across the wall of flesh. Between them all were teeth, the chittering maw running across the creature like alien runes. Tentacles sprouted from odd angles. To Helesys, it looked like a child's doll had been torn apart and sewn grisly back together.

Even though she stood as its equal in the mindspace, the kraken knew no fear—it had never known fear. It was from the far reaches of the universe, a place beyond even where the Idnauthi dwell. It might have even been from a place beyond—where the rules of time and space were different.

No, the kraken did not fear the weaver.

But as the heroes and the crab lurched through the hellish maelstrom of white flesh, it was testament to Helesys's power that she made the creature pause. For just a moment, a flicker of emotion passed over the creature, stuttering its onslaught and giving the heroes time to navigate and escape its grasp.

Not fear, but a flicker of something close—like a spark that hadn't caught flame.

The heroes sailed through the clutches of the beast and through more metal spires. Then the hull of the crab groaned again and then the whole of it lurched violently—

and fell.

Magic held them fast to their seats, but even still, Helesys's stomach turned at the sudden weightlessness. One hand gripped the arm of her chair and her metal hand pressed flat against the ceiling of the compartment. Instinctively, she turned her magic outward and bolstered her and Taunauk.

Metal spires raced by, and then the chalky mud of the bottom of the ocean grew large in their vision. Then there was a horrid thud as they struck the bottom. Impact racked the heroes, nearly tossing them from their seats—instead whipping them against the back of their seats.

The crab lurched to a stop, and Helesys could see nothing but sea bottom through the viewing window. Her head pounded. Salty air seeped in through somewhere in the breached hull—

For a moment, Helesys was dumbstruck by that realization. Air at the bottom of the ocean? She pressed a hand down to the floor to feel for water seeping in, but there was none. The inside of the crab was completely dry.

Taunauk was already rising, crouched in the confines. "Are you alright?"

She nodded. She stooped down and found a long gash in the hull from where they had hit the seafloor. Air seeped through.

"There's air," she whispered.

Taunauk grunted in affirmation, and a moment later he was pushing through the hatch and helping her out. The metal crab lay in a small crater of silt, the remnants of impact clouded the air. Beyond that lay darkness and the deep bellows of the kraken.

Helesys flared her warding light.

They were in a clearing, and beyond the settling silt, they were surrounded on three sides by spires. Beyond the towering metal lay the ocean—a mountain of water. The dark surface ebbed and shimmered like the ocean on a moonlit night.

She breathed deep. *Air*, Helesys thought again, marveling at the sight of it. They were at the bottom of the endless sea, yet within the confines of the grisly spires, there was air.

She thought back to One-Mind's realm and their battle with Dissimul—the mechanical god had used similar magic to keep the crushing water at bay.

A massive shadow grew in the wall of water, and the surface began to churn. The call of the monster grew deafening.

Helesys churned power and reveled in the comforting rattle of her metal arm.

Three snake-like tendrils reached out of the water, each even thicker than the spires. They twisted around the towers until they were nearly halfway across the clearing.

Helesys leveled her gauntlet, ready to fire, when the beast let out another dull groan. Then the tentacles retreated, slowly slithering back beneath the surface. The shadow disappeared as quickly as it arrived.

Helesys and Taunauk turned back to back, both scanning the water and the clearing for a surprise attack. For a long moment, neither moved nor spoke.

Taunauk grunted in annoyance. Helesys took his meaning, though he would not utter the words: *Too easy.*

~ ~ ~

The Bottom of the Endless Sea

Some minutes passed before the weaver and the barbarian relaxed their weapons. Helesys released most of her power until she felt the chill of the air. It was nowhere near as cold as the Godpeak, but she kindled strength and felt the chill subside.

"Come, let us find the abyssal machine," Taunauk said.

Helesys uttered the word to shrink the metal crab, then picked it up, dusted it off. Even shrunken, the legs of the poor contraption were bent and broken, though whole.

Her wand said quietly, *In time the crab will repair itself.* Helesys echoed this aloud for Taunauk, then pocketed the tiny contraption.

The heroes turned toward the silty path. The clearing stretched out beyond the edge of Helesys's warding light and was flanked with the spires, which stretched up more than a hundred feet and tapered off into the darkness.

They pressed forward into the gloom in silence, save for the occasional alien call or bellow of some hidden deep sea creature.

The spires seemed even larger and more numerous as they walked, soon giving way to other paths that branched off in various directions, like a cemetery to some incomprehensible gods. Despite the branching paths, Helesys felt the growing presence of magic—never doubting the path forward.

"What is this place?" Taunauk wondered aloud.

A few breaths later, realization dawned on the weaver. The spires were not haphazardly arranged, nor were the walking paths.

"They are runes," Helesys said reverently, "like those we saw from the Godpeak. Magic writ large and potent. This place is very old and built by skilled minds."

Taunauk grumbled. "It is humbling to walk through such a place. Even more so to find it empty."

Helesys felt weary as she craned her neck to follow the spires. The calls of sea life from beyond were growing quiet, as if the ocean were impossibly far away. There was nothing here, save for silt and lingering magic.

She whispered, "I hope the Voice on the beach was right about this place."

Taunauk asked, "The Machine of Antrikaumora… What do you think it does?"

"Whatever it is, it must be immensely powerful."

Taunauk snorted. "To be able to kill the Wolf King—I imagine it's quite powerful."

"It's not just that," Helesys said. "The Wolf King must know of its existence. He heard us in Amadeus's study when we merely breathed the wrong word."

"When we spoke of *her*." The Gatekeeper.

"Yes. So, why not destroy the Machine? If I were King, I would," she said.

"He cannot," Taunauk replied plainly. "So he hides it at the bottom of the ocean. Why let us find it then…"

Both Helesys and Taunauk slowed and turned back to back, weapons raised—neither needing to give breath to fate. The weaver's heart was beating in her throat. Power thrummed in her arm, a dozen spells ready to be uttered for the weaver didn't know which, if any, would save her. They circled, watching the path and the darkness beyond, waiting for an attack that did not come. It had to be a trap—it had to be.

"Show yourself," Taunauk growled.

But only silence answered.

"It doesn't make any sense," Taunauk said.

Helesys shook her head. "Perhaps we haven't sprung the trap yet. He doesn't know we are here." Helesys relaxed her power—only slightly. "Just because he is King does not mean he is omniscient. He must be watching Amadeus's study. Yes, that is how the Wolf King heard us."

As the weaver spoke, she didn't know who she was trying to convince more, Taunauk or herself.

Taunauk lowered his axe. "Could you find his trap before we stumble on it?"

Helesys nodded. "I think so. If it is magic, then I can find it. If it's not—"

"Then I will see it." Taunauk nodded reassuringly. Let us press forward then. A walk to ease my quaking chest."

~

Soon the spires had grown so numerous and towering that all trace of the deep sea was gone, save for the darkness and the smell of salt. They had walked in silence and stillness for long, and the weaver had felt nothing except for the subtle guidance of her wand. Her apprehension had waned. She sighed in muted comfort.

If there was a trap waiting for them, she was certain it would be closer to the source—closer to the resting place of the Machine of Antrikaumora.

"I've seen a twin of that creature before," Helesys said quietly. "There was a kraken trapped in the tunnels beneath the buried hive. It was… much smaller."

"I remember. I was nearly eaten a second time," Taunauk added with a smirk.

Helesys eyed her comrade. "Isn't that the Endroggen way, to die in glorious battle?"

"The goal of battle is not to die. It is for your enemy to die."

Helesys smiled. "You must admit, this must be some warrior's dream. What do your ancestors think of this place?"

For a moment, Taunauk's eyes glowed golden and his mouth twitched in silent whispers. He did not pause his strides across the silt.

When the glow faded, the barbarian said, "They are in agreement: There is no true death here, and so there is no true glory."

"What do you think?"

Taunauk glanced at her before turning his eyes back to the gloom. "I don't know what to think. My whole life I've been shaped into a vessel. I cannot die—not if I am to succeed in this task. There is no glorious death waiting for me, none equal to the task of saving the ten thousand lost."

Helesys replied, "Then there must be glory in life, in the struggle and in success. In *becoming* what we were meant to be."

Taunauk nodded. "There must be. It is purpose enough, for now."

Silence fell again, and Helesys contemplated his words. It felt as if they were on the Godpeak again, Taunauk amongst the souls of his father and the lost Endroggen, being denied the joys of youth, kinship, and partnership so that he could become the Vessel. Now he was denied even the glory of a barbarian death, for how could any battle eclipse this?

Helesys looked to her comrade, heart aching for him. "When we've wrested freedom from the Wolf King and delivered the souls of your people, we will find you a new purpose… Perhaps teaching the young ones how to master their rage."

Taunauk smiled, an emotion that smoldered in the harsh warding light. "That would be a noble task."

Though she wanted to say more, Helesys left it alone, for Taunauk's reply had been dutiful and cold.

One thing at a time, she reminded herself. It was impossible to see further than that in this place.

~

Some hours later, the metal spires were as thick and numerous as the giant trees of the wode. The paths between through became a maze, and Helesys knew that without the guidance of her wand, they would never have hoped to navigate it.

They came to a clearing—the largest yet—filled with squat mounds of silt. Spires stood at the edge of the warding light, as if even the towering metal was afraid to approach. The heroes stopped some forty feet away.

"More sorcery?" Taunauk asked quietly.

Helesys's wand hummed with warning. "Not likely," she muttered.

The mounds began to writhe, and serpentine shapes emerged. Its faces were little more than mouths full of rows of jagged teeth, arranged in four circles. its necks were muscular with skin that sagged loose beneath it. Behind the creature, a half-dozen arms ended in similar teeth-ringed faces.

Taunauk whispered, "The eels from the *Malorienta*." He stowed his ironwood shield and held his axe in both hands.

Helesys was already kindling power. She remembered all too well that frantic night hiding in the cargo hold and the grisly morning they awoke too. But here they did not have the luxury of hiding or funneling the creatures, nor could they even run, beset upon all sides by the crushing sea.

Dozens of the eels emerged from the mounds, but these were not the thin and lanky bodies of the creatures that attacked the ship in the night. These were as thick as pythons, and the ground shook as they woke. As dust clouded the air, it brought the musty smell of dried death.

"I mean to take as many as I can," Helesys said. Helesys dredged power and funneled it into her gauntlet, strengthening her body only enough to weather the blasts. Her warding light dimmed until she could barely see the creatures.

"Do it. We will take the rest."

Helesys released her power, and a dozen blasts of purple arcane energy sailed forth. Several of the beasts turned toward the oncoming fire, and a few even managed to twist out of the way; there were so many that the weaver's blasts struck true—thumps of silt and bursts of flesh echoed in the gloom.

She let loose a dozen more blasts before the creatures came for them, lumbering forth like nightmares-made-flesh. The fastest and smallest beasts skirted her blasts. The largest bar-reled through them, their flanks charred and bleeding.

The trickle of eels soon became a flood of writhing flesh and teeth, and Helesys kept firing. In the carnage, some stopped to eat their wounded.

Helesys felt the yearning of the Gar of Shéslang—that in-human thirst for battle—but she relented. An errant blast might damage the spires and too great a burst of power might alert the Wolf-King to their presence.

Instead, she called upon the Ring of Winter. She felt the telltale pinch of the icy tendril in her finger and her blasts took on its power—

But the eels pushed through, shrugging off the blasts. Helesys knew the flaw in her plan before her ring uttered the words:

They are creatures of the icy deep, and immune to the ring.

Taunauk roared, "Funnel them, Helesys!"

She was only vaguely aware of the golden warriors amassing around her.

Helesys pulled more power from the ring, and this time called forth a wall of ice. Painful frost swirled in her metal arm and several things happened all at once:

A stream of ice burst forth from her hand, creating a wall twice her height, a foot thick, and extending back into the spires—completely blocking the eels on their left. The rest of the eels reached them, and a dozen glowing warriors rushed forth to meet them.

Taunauk led the charge, filled with rage, and axe imbued with the magic of his father—golden swathes trailing in the violent afterglow. The warriors became a bulwark, a rocky shore on which the eels crashed and were mangled.

Helesys dove forward, somersaulting through the fray, and let loose one more icy blast. Another wall rose, this one cutting off the creatures to the right. Now the only way forward for the eels was through the narrow passage, barely enough for two of the larger beasts to clamber through. So far, the beasts had not been smart enough to double back and to around the blockades.

She split power into her body and her gauntlet, and then joined in the melee. With the Gar of Shéslang she split many and when the larger beasts reached her, she softened them with powerful spreadblasts from her gauntlet.

Thrice, an eel was able to scramble atop its brethren and over the icy wall. Helesys turned her gauntlet back to a ranged shot and burst them before they hit the ground.

The battle blurred to a whirlwind of steel, flesh, spirits, and arcane—roars of battle overshadowing the quiet of the seafloor. A cloud of silt grew and trailed behind each weapon.

As the heroes and spirits tore through the swarm of eels, they slowly backed away so that they did not have to fight amongst the still writhing and snapping piles of the dying.

Helesys lost track of time. For the briefest moment, she considered that she should dwell on Taunauk's first lesson of rage—that she and her weapons were separate. But she was lost in the fray—both a weaver and a soldier, unable to tell where body ended and spear or gauntlet began.

She merely *was*. And she reveled fighting alongside barbarians.

~

The eels' numbers dwindled in the fog of silk and battle until they were gone, and the battle was over. The last of them lay scattered across the ground, gnashing pitifully. Endroggen spirits had disappeared one by one along the dwindling number of enemies until only Helesys and Taunauk remained.

The weaver and barbarian relaxed and soon the fog settled. Both were covered in splatters of gray sludge—the mixture of blood and silt written on them like runes.

They strode silently through the carnage and between the icy barriers, avoiding those still writhing eels that hadn't the sense to die.

After they were past the battlefield, Helesys paused to look back. The carcasses were already dwindling, disappearing, re-incarnated to some other realm.

"Look," Taunauk said, pointing ahead.

In the distance, a mound of metal rose some thirty feet high and seemed to slope out twice as far. Strange runes covered the surface and the whole of it glistened in the light.

The hum of guidance from her wand grew strong as they approached.

Helesys asked her wand, *What spells are written on its surface?*

There are many. Most are spells of containment. Whatever is inside, the builders did not want it getting out. Most do not appear to be magical.

Helesys did not need her wand to elaborate. Slowly, she was able to recognize the inscriptions. Spells for grounding and non-location, and for hiding magic. The other inscriptions were blessings and curses in a language she could read but did not recognize. One of which was written larger than the rest:

Death hath made us weary. You who have walked a thousand lifetimes, let go the sleep of death and embrace eternity.

When they were nearly upon the structure, metallic scrapes and clanks sounded from within it, and both heroes readied their weapons. But instead of a trap, a seam emerged in the metal—a hidden door opened. The strange metal door gave way to a staircase.

Taunauk looked to her, and Helesys answered, "The Machine is here."

~ ~ ~

The Antechamber

Taunauk led them inside. As they descended the passage, their boots rang hollow on the metal, and light began to emanate dully from the surfaces. A few steps later, the doors clanked shut behind them.

Again, Helesys thought of One-Mind. She ended her warding light and whispered, "The machine god must have been here before. There are too many similarities between this place and its sanctum."

"Agreed."

"So, why didn't One-Mind take the Machine?"

Taunauk merely grunted thoughtfully, but offered nothing.

Helesys mused to herself. Perhaps One-Mind couldn't take the Machine. Or it is controlled by the mysterious Voice and meant only for the chosen. Perhaps even the power of the Machine was not a guarantee of success. Maybe One-Mind, Amadeus, and the other masters of the realms were simply afraid of dying and losing the progress they had struggled for—as they claimed.

And finally, the thought came to her: Perhaps One-Mind did not want to escape.

This gave the weaver pause; at first, it seemed ludicrous. Both One-Mind and Amadeus had sought escape by different means—a realm within a realm—but they were still within the dungeon.

Had a Terran ever sought the dungeon in the physical world as a means to live forever? She dismissed the notion as quickly as it came—if no one had escaped, how could anyone know the true nature of the prison?

The staircase stretched on. Runes and engravings lined the wall.

More spells of containment, her wand said.

"And more writings about death."

Taunauk paused and grunted in question.

"Sorry," Helesys muttered, not realizing she'd spoken aloud. "My wand says that these are spells of containment, but there are other inscriptions too. Blessings and writings about death."

"Anything about the Machine of Antrikaumora?"

Nothing yet, her wand said. Helesys echoed the words aloud.

They followed the staircase down, their steps ringing dully on the metal. Before long, the stairs wound back and forth, twisting and turning at odd angles.

The staircase itself is a rune of containment, her wand said. *You are nearly at the bottom.*

The temperature dropped further, and soon the heroes could see their breath. The weaver reached out a hand to touch the walls and found them icy to the touch, though no frost clung to the surface. As they neared the bottom, the sound of their footsteps on the metal grew deeper. It felt to Helesys like the hollowness had disappeared from beneath the metal.

The staircase ended and gave way to a maze. From the curving hallway in front of them, there were dozens of passageways.

"A labyrinth," Taunauk muttered. "Does your wand still guide you?"

I can feel the way, her wand said.

"Yes," Helesys replied to her comrade. Then she asked inwardly, More runes?

Yes, that is likely. But the layout is extraordinarily complex. I do not know what they mean.

The heroes pressed forward into the maze of hallways. The soft light emanating from the metal gave a perpetual twilight glow, and their steps echoed eerily down the corridors.

Though she hadn't felt the warning of her wand-arm, Helesys kindled strength and power. In front of her, Taunauk did the same, wielding Everfall and axe; golden smoke smoldering from his shoulders. Helesys could sense that they were close to the Machine, but such an artifact would not be unguarded—could not be unguarded. And in the strange architecture, Helesys had no idea what to expect.

All too soon, her suspicions were confirmed when they found two bodies lying motionless on the ground. The heroes approached wearily. Their leather armor was slashed through; dried blood was caked in the wounds and pooled beneath them in a thin tar.

Taunauk whispered, "The attack came from both sides. Their weapons are missing."

"Why are they still here?" Helesys asked, scanning the halls. "They should have been reborn somewhere else."

But Helesys and Taunauk already knew—her wand just gave voice to it:

This place prevents rebirth.

"Another lingering death," Taunauk mused.

From down the hall came a clacking sound and the thrum of strings, like a sitar plucked violently and out of tune. Helesys turned, gauntlet leveled, and saw a quickly approaching Terran form. It moved in drunken lurches, stumbling and bouncing against the wall. It wore the pinstripe suit and feathered hat of a jester—its clothes hanging loose in places they were cut and frayed from violence. Its arms ended in sickles instead of hands. Its face was blank—a deep ironwood carved vaguely in a Terran face.

Helesys let loose four arcane blasts, each striking true. The rest of the tattered clothes came free, smoldering in the air. The grisly construct lumbered unimpeded, its ironwood body scorched but otherwise unharmed.

The weaver narrowed her eyes and dredged power, bolstering her blasts further. These new shots collided and staggered the creature, but still it came.

Behind came the dull echo of steel on ironwood as Taunauk fought his own enemy—then the sound of a dozen more as Endroggen spirits sprang forth. The halls glowed a brilliant gold, but Helesys was only vaguely aware of the chaos unfolding in the labyrinth as dozens of the lifeless sculptures set upon them—

Her own foe was upon her and slashing with sickle hands. Helesys funneled her arcane might into her body and met the creature with the Gar of Shéslang. Tremors of impact wracked her arms and shoulders as the spear slashed wildly, becoming a blur of metal. But even as she batted away its weapons and struck its body, the ironwood was unphased. Behind her, Taunauk echoed similar frustration.

"We cannot break them!" he roared.

Helesys gritted her teeth and compounded her strength with that of the magic spear. Each impact of her spear became a thundercrack—became deafening—until the creature could scarcely lift its arms in defense.

But as her strength swelled, Helesys began to doubt. No matter her power, the creature's ironwood body would not crack or dent. Nor would the creature stumble and fall to its knees.

Worse, she felt as if her powers were dulled, as if the magic-laden walls of the labyrinth were suppressing them somehow.

It wasn't until Helesys channeled her full might into a single blow, bringing the spear down heavy across the creature's neck and shoulder, that she saw it waiver for the first time: The body shuddered, and above it Helesys saw a slender string running from the ceiling to the neck of the creature—saw the string snap. The creature staggered to its knees, and all at once, Helesys saw the vague shimmers of a dozen strings running from the surrounding metal to the ironwood limbs and body of the creature like a violent marionnette.

Before the thing could come for her, Helesys swung the spear high toward the other strings. Even with her power, she snapped only two before it lashed out again with sickles.

Burn them, Helesys, came the quiet voice of her wand. *Burn them all.*

The weaver struck the mannequin once more and sent it staggering backward on its cut strings. Then she turned her power toward her fire spell.

"Ignis flores."

A veil of fire blossomed from her gauntlet and washed over the marionette. Before it could slash again, the strings caught fire and severed, and the thing dropped lifelessly to the ground.

Helesys stared at it only a moment to be certain it was lifeless before she turned to the others.

For as powerful as the *fire blossom* spell was, it should've been more potent.

Again she dredged power, knowing that she would have to call on her full might to put an end to the battle.

"Fall back to me!" she shouted, and then, "Taunauk, bolster yourself!"

Taunauk and the golden warriors backed toward her in the center of the hall and their formation grew tight.

"Now," Taunauk roared, and drew the golden warriors back into himself. He blazed with a golden light and became a blur as he fought with the ferocity of a dozen Endroggen.

"*Ignis flores!*" Helesys waved her arms and an inferno burst forth, bathing the halls in flames. There was a sudden sparkle as the strings of the marionettes singed and they dropped to the floor.

As violent as the explosion was, the flames fizzled and died when they were no more than ten feet away.

In the quiet aftermath, Taunauk looked to his weapons and his hands and found his golden glow flickering and unsteady.

"You feel it too," Helesys said. "Something is dulling our magic." She lowered her gauntlet and breathed deep. The air smelled sweet and burnt.

Taunauk said, "My connection to my ancestors... They are still there, but their voices are faint."

There was a sadness in his voice: That of a man who had gone to the ends of the world and given his life several times over to find his father and his ancestors, and who did not want to lose them. Not so soon.

"It's something in this place—nothing more," she said reassuringly. "Once we leave, you will hear them clearly again."

Taunauk nodded reluctantly, and the glow faded from him. After a moment, he led them over the now lifeless piles of ironwood and down the hall.

~

They walked the halls with weapons ready, weary of any more of the grisly constructs, but they found only silence and bodies of the lingering dead.

Helesys felt the magic warning growing fainter by the step. She flared her warding light to test this, and found that even with dredging her power, the light only extended faintly into the hall. Soon it did nothing more than flicker and light her face. She imagined that her blasts and other projections would be similarly weak.

Even her sense of direction was dulled, and Helesys found herself asking her wand for guidance more as they pressed deeper into the labyrinth.

The only thing she felt unchanged was her kindled strength. It felt as if whatever strange properties of this place dulled magic could not nullify the magic contained in her body.

Helesys asked quietly, "What about your rage?"

Taunauk walked in silence a moment before answering, "My rage is untouched, even now."

"I think this place nullifies magic. That is why my blasts are weak and your ancestors are quiet. The further we walk, the more I'm certain that same property hides this place from the Wolf King."

Taunauk considered this, then added, "And that is why One-Mind did not take the Machine for itself. The machine god is pure magic and could not come this far. There is a problem…"

"What is that?"

"Once we take the Machine of Antrikaumora from this place, it will no longer be hidden. What if the Wolf King can see it and find us?"

Helesys had considered this, but simply shrugged—a gesture that Taunauk could not see as he walked ahead. "Then our battle will come early."

Her comrade grunted in satisfaction.

~

The walls began to change and warp. Engravings disappeared, and gave way to protrusions. These rose out of the wall in regular patterns, lengthening until they were spikes nearly a foot long—four-sided and geometric. The ceiling and walls seemed to widen slightly to accommodate the spikes.

"What in Movernus's name…" Taunauk trailed off. As he spoke, his words fell empty on the walls, and even his footsteps fell only once. The telltale echo and reverberation of the metal hall was gone. "What sorcery is this?"

Helesys eyed the walls as they stretched off in either direction. The maze-like corridors were gone, replaced by passages arranged in rings around a central point.

Her wand said quietly, *The spikes dissipate noise. These passages seem to surround the central chamber, hiding any sound from within.*

Helesys asked internally, *Why would they need to do this?*

I do not know why, but clearly they felt it necessary, Helesys.

Finally, Helesys said to Taunauk, "The spikes are harmless. They merely dampen sound."

But as she spoke, Helesys's stomach turned. There was something eerie and alien about the lack of an echo, as if she and Taunauk were utterly alone in this strange place so far beneath the endless sea. So alone that the walls themselves did not acknowledge them.

Taunauk eyed the walls suspiciously before motioning for them to continue. "Come. I grow weary of this realm."

~ ~ ~

The Vault

Sometime later, the spiked passageway ended. The walls became sleek again, and engraved with the same containment runes. And with it, sound returned.

From down the halls came the sliding and clangs of metal—the sound of machinery. Helesys's mind flashed back to the city of Novissimé and machines great and small that worked to keep magic flowing through it.

But as the heroes walked and left the spikes behind completely, the whine of machinery grew to squeals and screams—high-pitched agony that Helesys bolstered herself to withstand. Even Taunauk paused, his golden glow returning to shield him from the onslaught.

They walked through a single short corridor that ended at a door. It was circular and squat, barely tall enough for Helesys, and made of the same sleek, engraved metal as the earlier halls.

What does the runes say? Helesys asked her wand.

They are all containment runes—the same as those written on the walls before. These are the same spells repeated over and over. Only the mantle above the door is different.

Helesys glanced upward and saw rough engravings, that which might've been scoured by a blade yet with a smooth hand.

It says: Only the Chosen may proceed. By the will of Sinatin Koh."

Helesys stepped forward and Taunauk stepped aside, eyeing her and the door wearily. The weaver held up her gauntlet, running her metal fingers over the sleek metal of its surface.

Show me how to open it, she commanded.

So, the wand said, and Helesys repeated aloud:

"I have become a master of life, such that no death can sate me. But there is a power even greater—

"Behold the Machine of Antrikaumora! That which makes gods tremble.

"I have become a master of fate as well."

Even though Helesys's voice boomed as she spoke, she could barely hear herself over the screams of metal. When she finished, the doors snapped open, spinning outward violently and disappearing into the metal of the structure.

Helesys winced as the metallic scraping grew impossibly loud. She dredged power to bolster herself and the world went silent.

When she opened her eyes, she saw another hallway—a tunnel—beyond the door, except that this one was moving. Instead of walls or a ceiling or a floor, gears lined the passageway, whirling around it at impossible speed. Helesys stared, but found the mechanisms so volatile and confusing that she couldn't follow them—the more she stared the more they looked like whirling spikes or claws.

At the end, some fifty feet away, was an equally vicious looking clockwork sphere, spinning with the same violent intensity as the hallway.

Slowly, she became aware of something else—the utter decimation of magic. It felt as if a noxious cloud poured from the hallway, an invisible smoke that seemed to extinguish all magic, save for that bound within Helesys's own body. To the weaver, one who had spent all the life she could remember counting on such magic, defending herself and cloaking herself in it, the lack of magic felt as if she were stripped bare and defenseless. She shivered and pulled her gauntlet close.

Even Taunauk stood transfixed on the unholy sight.

A metal platform extended from the doorway, stretching across the hall, and forming a small platform around the spinning sphere.

Her wand asked, *Do you feel it, Helesys? There lies the Machine.*

Even with magic bolstering her, Helesys had to force herself to step toward the walkway.

Taunauk seized her metal arm, startling her. Though it was too loud to speak, she read his face clearly. He was wracked with concern. If he were to fall here, without the chance of reincarnation, his people would be lost forever.

So, Helesys pointed to herself, and gestured that she would cross the platform and that Taunauk should stay.

He stared at her with an intensity Helesys rarely seen aside from battle, and finally he let go of her arm. For a moment, she considered that he was worried for her too, but there was no other choice.

The only way to escape was to defeat the Wolf King, and they required the Machine to do that.

Slowly, Helesys stepped onto the walkway. The metal was so thin that she expected it to flex under her weight, but it held impossibly firm. She walked across, and as she became surrounded by the whirring, spinning machinations, the sight grew dizzying. She felt the void of magic grow heavy and oppressive, as if the very absence of magic might weigh her down and suffocate her.

Even when she'd finally crossed the path and stood in front of the sphere, she still felt that void.

She stared at the impossible, spinning contraption—rings upon rings of spinning energy, somehow kept in place without magic. And in the center, a tiny cube, only visible in glimpses as the machinery spun around it.

And Helesys began to doubt what she was supposed to do.

"Only the Chosen…" she muttered, and the words fell silently from her lips, overshadowed by the deafening roar of metal. "But there have been other Chosen."

Yes there have, came her wand's quiet answer.

Questions flashed through Helesys's mind: *Has the Voice on the beach spoken to others? Did other Chosen know about the Machine? How is it still here waiting for us?*

Perhaps Sinatin Koh is the Voice, and you are his last hope.

But why us? Helesys asked.

I know as little as you, her wand replied. *This is the path forward. Proclaim who you are and take your prize.*

Her wand helped, and Helesys echoed the words aloud. "I am Helesys Byyra, one of the Chosen, and I claim the Machine of Antrikaumora."

For a moment, Helesys felt her bolstered strength ebb, and silence gave way horrid screeching as the sounds of whirring gears came back to the Helesys's world. She winced and covered her ears. Thankfully, her strength returned, the noise diminished and grew bearable again. She looked upon the sphere and found the rings slowing until their revolutions halted completely.

The tiny cube lay in the center for her to take—small enough to fit in her palm. Its surface was covered in runes set with deep red inlay, the color of blood and power. Even still, Helesys could sense something potent within it—something magnitudes greater than she'd felt with any other relic.

She reached out with her metal hand. So close to the Machine, her arm grew numb, and when she grasped the cube and pulled it free, she could feel nothing in her hand at all.

The screeching metal of the facility diminished further, and she turned to find the deathly gears of the hallway slowing to a halt. As the sounds faded, Helesys felt magic returning to the word—felt the magic that coursed through the metal walls and strange architecture.

All at once, she understood what the Machine of Antrikaumora was meant to do—why her gauntlet still worked though she could feel nothing through its metal skin; why she could bolster herself, yet her magic fizzled in the open air; why the marionettes were bound by tethers and lifeless when cut; and finally, why her wand still spoke, yet Helesys could not feel the subtle pushes, pulls, and urges—

The Machine emitted an anti-magic field. It stifled magic from leaving the body and the surfaces from which it was born.

It was the ultimate weapon against a weaver, against the Wolf King. The ability to take power from another, and render them mortal. To rend a god.

There was a singular, immense crash above them. Something impossibly distant that shook the entire facility.

Helesys reached out her metal hand to the wall to steady herself and felt the metal groaning—felt the power of the place fading. The facility had been built to hide and stifle the Machine like a giant mirror, but also used its power to repel the sea above. And without its power source, the crushing weight of the sea had dropped down on them and was already forcing its way inside the metal through a hundred slivers and pinprick holes.

As she felt this, she also felt hole left by the Machine—a tear in the world. A seam.

Helesys turned and shouted, "To me!"

Taunauk sprinted across the walkway, half-glowing with power.

Behind him, a low whistle sounded through the halls like eerie music. Before the barbarian had crossed the walkway, the whistle had grown to a roar. The smell of salt followed.

Helesys was already reaching for the seam and prying it open. A dozen worlds flickered across her mind's eye and she had no time to sort them.

She and Taunauk stepped through the portal as waves poured through the hall, burying the facility beneath the endless sea.

~

Helesys and Taunauk stepped into a barren field. The ground was blistered and cracked beneath their boots, and the sky bled red above them. Hot wind blew across the land, bringing the faint smell of dust and earth.

The pair surveyed the land, and when they found no immediate danger, they relaxed, if only slightly.

Taunauk asked, "Do you sense our next direction?"

"This is not the Wolf King's realm," she replied. "I didn't have time to look for it."

Helesys scanned the horizon and felt the quiet direction of her wand return. Once again, she could feel its influence

Her wand said, *It was the Machine of Antrikaumora. Being so near it while its aura was active prevented you from sensing me. I was forced to speak to you directly.*

Helesys replied internally, *Glad to have you back.*

Then she turned to Taunauk's question. She felt the wand's subtle guidance directing them over the desert. As she faced that direction, a bright beam of yellow light appeared—shooting up from some point beyond the horizon and up into the sky.

"Is that it?" Taunauk asked.

"Yes," Helesys replied wearily. "That is the next seam."

"Very well," the barbarian said, striding forward with Everfall and axe in hand.

Helesys followed.

~ ~ ~

NEXT TIME ON
*A BATTLEAXE AND
A METAL ARM*
Book 14:

Test of Faith
Available May 2022

Spoiler–Free excerpt from *BAMA 14*

They walked for hours, though in the perpetual sunset they had no idea of knowing just how long had passed.

Twice, zombies rose from the ground. The first group were Terran, a shambling, sprawling mass of hundreds—nothing compared to the group that had surrounded Shawn upon his first arrival. The three heroes tore through the undead horde like sickles through wheat. Shawn became a blur, while Taunauk and his Endroggen spirits sprawled out across the field.

Meanwhile, Helesys called on her arcane blasts and spear. She reached for her memories of her mother and her sister, and tried to harness the power of rage.

But each time she thought of something other than battle—each time she thought of anything at all—it felt as if her blasts flew errantly, and her spear didn't quite strike true. Truth be it that the zombies were so numerous that even an errant blast killed something, and they were so weak that even a mistimed strike broke them in two, but Helesys noticed.

She knew there was power in Endroggen rage, yet for her it seemed merely a distraction. The weaver grew frustrated with herself. So much else came easily: Spells came to memory when they were needed, fighting maneuvers too. But Endroggen blood magic eluded her that battle.

When zombies appeared the second time, the mottled, rotting flesh was the only thing that was similar. Their shapes were strange. The Terrans that rose were misshapen or asymmetrical—one arm longer than the rest, hands as big as torsos, or uneven legs that gave them a horrific, galloping gait, and those were the least strange. Others had wings, the skin long since sloughed off so that they looked like long, gnarled fingers. Others were gargantuan, four-legged beasts that had never been Terran, but were far too decomposed to tell what they might've been before. They crawled from the ground and lumbered on ragged limbs, some without even muscle or ligaments to move them—

Helesys churned power and thought of the bonemen from the cannibals' realm. Foul magic steeped this desert.

To be continued May 2022

Thank you for Reading

I hope you enjoyed reading this story as much as I enjoyed writing it.

If you did, I would massively appreciate a short review on Amazon or your favorite book website. Reviews are crucial for any author, and a starred review or even just a line or two can make a huge difference.

It's especially true for the start of a series. Thanks and I hope you enjoy the next one!

Looking for more Engrossing Fantasy?

You might like ***Tales from Another World,*** an ongoing short story series containing stories about sorcerers, druids, mortals, gods, thieves, and all other manner of Terrans.

The 2nd and 3rd installments are out and they tie into the outside world of *A Battleaxe and a Metal Arm.* So, if you're looking for more engrossing fantasy stories, and if you want to know more about this fantasy universe, read on and see how deep the rabbit hole goes.

What questions do you have about *A Battleaxe and a Metal Arm*?

If you've read this far, hopefully you'll read a bit further—both in this book and across the series. I'm not sure how most authors write serials and how much of it is flying by the seat of their pants, but that's not how I do things. For all the major questions that might come up in BAMA, I already have answers for 95% of them. Same goes for the major plot points, twists and climaxes. That might sound boring to some, especially some of you other authors who enjoy variations of writing into the dark, but I think having a solid blueprint is paramount to writing a long series.

So, what questions do you have about the story? Here are a few:

1) ~~What is the dungeon?~~ It's a soul trap of overwhelming size and power. But where did it come from? Is it a force of nature or an ill-made weapon, or perhaps something else entirely? In the real world, it looks like a giant cloud with faces writhing just beneath the surface. Helesys speculates that the

reason no one remembers it is because it's so horrific their minds blot it out!

2) ~~Who was Helesys before she got trapped~~? We've learned that Helesys was both a soldier and was the oldest daughter of the elven Great House Byyra.

3) ~~Who was Taunauk before he got trapped~~? There was an omen of a blight in the Endroggen heaven, Accaelum. Taunauk is an Endroggen barbarian who was raised as a warrior and a vessel. His purpose was to one day free the trapped Endroggen souls from the Dungeon.

4) How well did they know each other beforehand?

5) How did Helesys get her metal arm? Likely through injury, amputation, and replacement. She was likely fighting in the Eternal War, the war of the Elves against the Shadowkind.

6) ~~Who is Shawn~~? He is a wisp from the plane of dreams. One who walks through the dreams of elves and humans, while being neither. He has lived as both a god and a mortal.

7) Why does Shawn feel so familiar to Helesys and Taunauk? The group speculates that they were traveling together for unknown reasons. Shawn worries that they were tracking him. This could explain why Helesys and Taunauk are always reborn together, while Shawn was usually alone.

7) Who is the Wolf King and what sinister plans does he have for our heroes? How did he come to rule over the Dungeon? How does the Gatekeeper factor into all this?

8) Who is the mysterious voice encountered on the white sandy shores of Meridian? Why do they seek the death of the Wolf-King? ...And why did they choose the heroes?

Did I miss any questions? Probably. Connect with me and other *BAMA* fans on social media and compare questions!

I've got plans. I've got answers. And I've got them on a drip-feed. Keep reading and expect to find out a little more to the mysteries with each installment. Hopefully, you're as excited about this series as I am.

Connect with the Author

If you want to stay up to date on the latest about Samuel's publishing news and blog, check out his website and consider signing up for his monthly newsletter.

www.SamuelFlemingBooks.com

Samuel can also be found on Reddit, Goodreads and Facebook.

Samuel Fleming is a Science Fiction and Fantasy author.
He grew up in Maryland, spending most of his time swimming and writing. Swimming gave him a lot of time to daydream, so the two hobbies complemented each other well. Idle day dreams turned into stories, some of which stuck with him for years. These days he swims a little less and writes a lot more.
He loves a good story no matter the medium: Books, TV, video games, comics, tabletop RPG's, or podcasts–most of which he attempts to share with his wife and three kids, and occasionally on his blog.